A

ENVY

ENVY

A NOVEL

KATHRYN HARRISON

 RANDOM HOUSE • NEW YORK

Copyright © 2005 by Kathryn Harrison

Published in the United States by Random House, an imprint of The Random House Publishing Group, a division of Random House, Inc., New York.

RANDOM HOUSE and colophon are registered trademarks of Random House, Inc.

Library of Congress Cataloging-in-Publication Data

Harrison, Kathryn.
Envy: a novel / Kathryn Harrison.
p.   cm.
ISBN 1-4000-6346-9
1. Middle aged men—Fiction. 2. Psychoanalysts—Fiction. 3. Class reunions—Fiction. 4. Midlife crisis—Fiction. 5. Sex addiction—Fiction. 6. Sons—Death—Fiction. 7. Brothers—Fiction. 8. Twins—Fiction. I. Title.
PS3558.A67136E58 2005
813'.54—dc22   2004061429

Printed in the United States of America on acid-free paper

9 8 7 6 5 4 3 2 1

www.atrandom.com

First Edition

Book design by Susan Turner

for Kate Medina

In those years I had a great need to be seen.
And when one succeeds in seducing someone,
one also succeeds in being seen.

—Lars Gustafsson,
  The Death of a Beekeeper

ENVY

W ill leans out of the driver's-side window toward his wife. "It's not too late to change your mind," he says.

Her dark glasses show him the houses on their side of the block, greatly reduced and warped by the convexity of each lens. The fancy wrought-iron bars on their neighbor's windows, the bright plastic backboard of the Little Tikes basketball hoop one door down, the white climbing rose, suddenly and profusely in bloom, on the trellis by their own mailbox: it's as if he were studying one of those jewel-like miniatures painted in Persia during the sixteenth century; the longer Will looks, the more tiny details he finds.

"Did you remember to bring pictures?" Carole asks.

He points to an envelope on the seat beside him. "I mentioned the pool at the hotel?"

"Several times."

"Babysitting services? Pay-per-view?"

"Come on, Will," Carole says, "don't do this to me."

"Do what?"

"Make me feel guilty." Her bra strap has slipped out from the armhole of her sleeveless dress, down one shoulder. Without looking, she tucks it back where it belongs.

"You know I'd make it up to you," he tells her. She smiles, raises her eyebrows so they appear above the frames of her sunglasses.

"And how might you do that?" she asks him.

"By being your sex slave."

She reaches behind his neck to adjust his collar. "Aren't you forgetting something?" she says.

"What's that?"

"You already are my sex slave."

"Oh," Will says, "right." The errant strap has reemerged, a black satiny one he recognizes as belonging to the bra that unhooks in front.

Carole ducks her head in the window to brush her lips against his cheek, a kiss, but not quite: no pucker, no sound. For a moment she rests her forehead against his. "I just can't deal with it. You know that. I can't talk about Luke—not with people I don't know. And the same goes for your brother." She pulls back to look at him. "If you weren't such a masochist, you wouldn't be going either."

I'm curious, Will thinks of saying. *It's not as simple as masochism. Or as complicated.* Carole steps back from the car door.

"See you Sunday," she says, and her voice has returned to its previous playful tone. "Call if you get lonely."

"Oh, I doubt that'll be necessary." Will turns the key in the ignition. "I'll be too busy connecting with old friends. Blowing on the embers of undergraduate romance . . ."

"Checking out the hairlines," she says. "Seeing who got fat and who got really fat."

Will glances in the rearview mirror as he drives away, sees his wife climb the stairs to their front door, the flash of light as she opens it, the late June sun hot and yellow against its big pane of glass.

Something about the cavernous tent defeats acoustics: the voices of the class of '79, those Cornell alumni who made it back for their twenty-fifth reunion, combine in a percussive assault on the eardrum, the kind Will associates with driving on a highway, one window cracked for air, that annoying *whuh-whuh-whuh* sound. He moves his lower jaw from side to side to dispel the echoey, dizzy feeling. Psychosomatic, he concludes. Why is he here, anyway? Does he even want to make the effort to hear well enough to engage with these people? Everyone around him, it seems, isn't talking so much as advertising. Husbands describing vacations too expensive to include basic plumbing, referring to them as experiences rather than travel, as in "our rain forest experience." And, as if to demonstrate what good sports they are, wives laughing at everything, including comments that strike Will as pure information. "No, they relocated." "Ohio, wasn't it?" "The kids are from the first marriage." "She fell in love with this guy overseas."

He tries to picture the women's workaday selves: quieter, with paler lips, flatter hair. Still, on the whole they're well preserved, while the men by their sides look worn and rumpled. Receding hairlines have nowhere else to go; love handles have grown too big to take hold of.

"Hey!" someone says, and Will turns around to a face he remembers from his freshman dorm. "David Snader!" the face bellows to identify itself. With his big, hot hand, David pulls Will into a crushing hug. "Where you been!" he says, as though he'd lost track of Will hours rather than decades ago.

"Hey!" Will pulls out of the sweaty and, it would appear, drunken embrace.

"Are you here alone?" David asks him. He blots his forehead with a handkerchief.

Will nods. "Carole—my wife—she wasn't up for a long weekend of nostalgia with people she's never met before."

"Same here. Same here." David gives Will a companionable punch in the arm. "Where's Mitch?" he asks, and Will shrugs.

"Didn't make it. At least not as far as I know."

"Oh yeah?" David squints. "You guys not in touch or something?"

"Not at the moment."

"Well." He punches Will's arm again. "Guess that makes sense. All the travel. Media. Price of fame."

Will produces the rueful smile he hopes will convey that his estrangement from his famous twin is no big deal. Unfortunate, of course, but nothing hurtful or embarrassing. He's about to ask David about his wife and whether or not they have children, when David lurches off into the crowd. Will fills his cheeks with air, blows it out in a gust. David Snader is the fifth person in one hour to have approached him to ask not about Will or Will's work, his family, but about his brother, whose career as a long-distance swimmer has given Mitch a name as recognizable as that of, say, Lance Armstrong or Tiger Woods. Not that any of these alumni were his friends. Will and David hadn't even liked each other. But still.

He goes to the bar for a glass of red wine. If he's going to drink, he might as well rinse a little cholesterol out of his arteries. He's just replacing his wallet in the inside breast pocket of his blazer when he looks up to see someone else bearing down on him, Sue Shimakawa, with whom he'd shared an exam-week tryst, if that's the right word for abbreviated coitus in the musty, rarely penetrated stacks of the undergraduate library. Punch-drunk from studying chemistry for a few hundred hours, on a dare Will had asked Sue to have sex with him, prepared for a slap, or for her badmouthing him later or laughing at him in the moment, anything but what he got: her accepting his invitation with a sort of gung-ho enthusiasm. She had one of those bodies Will thinks of as typically Asian: compact, androgynous, and smooth-skinned, with pubic hair that was absolutely straight instead of curly, the surprise of this discovery—along with the panic induced by having intercourse in a potentially public place—enough to eclipse other, more inclusive observations.

"Will, Will, Will," Sue sings at him. "I was hoping to see you!" She has a man in tow, a sandy-haired giant at least a foot and a half taller than she. "Meet Rob. We have five kids, if you can believe it! Five!"

Wow, Will is about to say when Sue turns to her husband and says, "Rob, this is Will Moreland, an old fuck-buddy of mine."

Whether Rob is mute or only, like Will, horrified into silence, he thrusts his big, freckled hand forward without saying a word. The two men shake, silent in the clamor all around them, and then each drops his hand to his side and looks at Sue to see what might happen next.

"Rob's a debt analyst," she says.

"Really!" Will exclaims.

"Yes."

They all nod.

"Hey, hey," Sue says. "How about that brother of yours, huh? We're major fans. Major."

"He has had a spectacular ride." For once, Will is relieved when the conversation turns to his brother.

"Oh, I don't know. There's heaps of athletes that are celebrities."

"Of course, yes," Will says. "I know that. I just—"

"Is he here?"

"Here?"

"At the reunion. Here at the reunion."

"No. I'm afraid not."

"Oh, too bad. I really wanted to catch a glimpse of him."

Me, too, Will thinks as Sue and her husband move off. Having not heard from his brother for fifteen years now, during which time Mitch went from being known in the world of elite swimmers to being known by just about everyone, Will fantasized that Mitch might actually show up. If he's honest with himself, the hope of seeing his brother was at least part of what persuaded him to attend the reunion—especially after he'd learned that Andrew Goldstein, the one friend with whom he'd kept in touch after college, wouldn't be coming because his wife's due date fell on the same weekend. Not that seeing Mitch would be pleasant or, Will imagines, anything less than traumatic, but he's fed up with having to manage his private anguish even as he's forced to admit sheepishly to friends, colleagues, neighbors, and now alumni that he's no better informed about his brother's latest stunt swim—as Will has come to think of them—than the average reader of *Sports Illustrated.*

"Hello," says a voice behind him, startling Will out of what Carole would call one of his social desertions, when he becomes a spectator rather than a participant. He turns in the direction of the flirtatious tone he almost recognizes. As for the face: arresting, angular, unforgettable. Thinner than she used to be, but no less substantial—she looks concentrated, a distillate of her younger self.

"Elizabeth," he says.

"William." She tilts her head to one side, lifts her eyebrows. "Were you looking for someone?"

"You, of course. Who else?" Will unbuttons his shirt collar and loosens his tie. "Do you think I didn't scour each of those e-mail bulletins listing who was planning to attend, hoping—hoping against hope—to see your name?"

"Can it be?" Elizabeth says. "Has Mr. Fatally Earnest developed a sense of humor?"

"Only in extremis."

Elizabeth glances around herself. "I guess this qualifies," she says.

"Actually, I was just looking over the crowd. Seeing what generalizations I could make about the class of 'seventy-nine."

"And?"

He shrugs. "I don't know that I've had enough time to study my impressions. You?"

She shakes her head. "Insufficient data," she says.

"Data? That's a clinical word."

"I'm a clinician."

"Oh, right. I'd heard you'd gone on to med school." Having read her bio in the reunion book—studied it would not be inaccurate—Will knows also to which school Elizabeth went, when she got her degree, and where she now works. But he's not going to give her the (false) impression that he's still pining for her. "Where'd you end up—what school?" he asks.

"Johns Hopkins." Elizabeth pauses, Will suspects, to give him the opportunity to compliment her for having been accepted by a top-flight med school. He dips his head in an abbreviated bow of congratulation. "I was in dermatology," she continues, "then I specialized."

"I thought being a dermatologist was specializing."

"It is. It is up to a point. I went further, into burn treatment. I'm the program head at Johns Hopkins. We get patients from all over. Medevacked." Another pause. This time Will holds up his glass as if to begin a toast.

"So," he says, "no clinical observations whatsoever?"

She takes a sip from her drink. "The usual midlife stuff. Sun damage mostly, keratosis, a few carcinomas. But you probably weren't talking pathology, were you?" She looks around the big tent, shrugs. "Standard nip and tuck," she says. "Eyes. Neck. This isn't exactly a B-and-C crowd."

"B-and-C?"

"Botox and collagen." She draws her eyebrows together as she turns her attention back to him. "You?" she asks.

"Nah. Well, not collagen anyway. Maybe some Botox when I hit fifty."

Elizabeth ignores this. "I was wondering what it is that you do," she says.

"I'm a shrink."

"Really?" She smiles a faintly condescending smile. Will remembers this about her, the superior manner she wouldn't get away with were she less attractive.

"Really," he says.

"You look the part."

"Do I? How?"

"Oh, you know, the beard, the glasses. And you always did have those deep-set eyes that make you look thoughtful. How's Mitch?" she asks, moving efficiently through the expectable topics. "Is he here? I don't have to ask what he's been up to."

"He didn't make it, I'm afraid."

"Is he avoiding you?"

"What's that supposed to mean?"

"Nothing," she says, but she looks at him diagnostically, he thinks.

"Can I get you another drink?"

"Sure," she says. She hands him her glass. "Gimlet," she tells him. "Vodka, not gin."

"Why don't you grab that table before someone else does?"

When Will returns, Elizabeth has taken off her shoes and is sitting with one leg tucked under herself. She's one of those women, it strikes him, who will remain indefinitely athletic and limber—a woman like his wife, actually.

"So," she says. "Were you at the tenth?"

He shakes his head. "I was getting married. You?"

"Nope. Traveling."

"Somewhere good?"

"Cape Town. A conference. I managed to tack on a few days." She takes a sip from her glass, frowns, stirs it with a finger. "What have you been up to for the last twenty-five years, William? You didn't submit one of those what-I-did-over-summer-vacation reports. How come?"

"I don't know. Missed the deadline, I guess."

"Still married?" she asks.

He nods.

"She's not here?"

"She hates reunions."

Elizabeth smiles. "Me, too," she says. "Kids?"

"Two. Boy. Then a girl." He takes a breath. "The boy died," he says, amazed as always at how the words just come out. *The boy died.* Like any other little sentence. The boy climbed. The boy jumped. The boy ate his dinner.

"Oh, William. I'm—I'm so sorry. I had . . ." She talks through the hand covering her mouth. "I had no idea."

"No. How could you? That's the real reason I didn't send in the bio. I couldn't get around that one piece of news."

"When? When did he . . . when did it happen?"

"Three summers ago. An accident at a lake." Will looks at her and she looks away, briefly, then returns her eyes to his. "It's . . . we don't need to talk about it," he says, and he takes a swallow of his wine. "Among the things I didn't anticipate about death was how awkward a subject it is. Just mentioning it is the equivalent of a terrible gaffe, like pouring your drink on someone or inadvertently exposing yourself. An inappropriate nakedness. You just can't . . . people can't get past it. But, well, I find it equally impossible not to bring it up."

Elizabeth slips back into her shoes and stands. "I have an idea. I'll go to the women's room. I think it's over there." She points in the direction of a nondescript building, he can't remember what it is, a library maybe. "It'll give us an intermission, sort of. Then you can . . . we can . . . well, we can start over. Or not. You decide."

Will watches her move through the crowd, nimble and quick, as if she's trained for this specific topography, the congested party. Alone at the table, he finds the level of noise around him almost intolerable, one voice indistinguishable from another, punctuated by bursts of loud, alcohol-fueled laughter. He's glad to be slightly drunk himself; it makes it easier to move on from Luke to another topic.

"I want to ask you something," he says when Elizabeth sits back down in the chair opposite his. She inclines her head very slightly in a gesture of assent, nothing so unequivocal as a full nod. Her face is untanned, the freckles she had in college gone, bleached away perhaps, and her eyebrows are thicker now, almost lush. They balance the new, more tense and defiant line of her jaw.

"You left me in 1979." Will stops to consider what he's just said. Context, context, he warns himself: college reunion, level of blood alcohol, his tendency to make interpersonal missteps in Carole's absence. Anger, too, still there, not quite burnt out. A mistake to ignore it, even if it is a given. It seems Elizabeth's ability to provoke him, to knock him off-kilter, hasn't diminished. If anything, it's more intense, just like the rest of her. Ironic that she'd become a dermatologist. She'd always had a personality like a rash, itchy, chafing, the kind of woman who just won't let you get comfortable. A waiter moves among the tables, gathering abandoned glasses onto a tray.

Elizabeth brushes her hair back with obvious irritation. "We're not—that's not what we're going to talk about, is it?" she says.

"No," he says. "We're not."

"Okay, good. Look, I'm sorry. But . . ." She's shaking her head. "I don't want to talk about our breaking up when we were, what, however old we were twenty-five years ago."

"You were twenty-one."

"Not quite," she says.

"And I was twenty-two."

"Twenty-two," she agrees.

"And then you married."

"I did."

"You had a child."

"Yes."

Will nods. "I read your bio," he says. "No pictures, though. Did you bring any? Any pictures of her?"

"No. Well, I have one, but it's back in my room."

"She's how old?"

"Jennifer?"

"Jennifer."

Elizabeth produces her hands from under the table and places them together below her chin, palms and fingers aligned as if in prayer. A pretty gesture, it makes him wonder if she prays, goes to church, believes in God. Did she used to? He can't remember. "Oh," she says, nodding. "I get it. I get it now."

"Get what?" he says.

Mouth closed, she looks as if she might be holding her breath, counting to ten so as not to lose her temper. Her face is every bit as arresting as it was when they were students together. More so, because the passage of years has scrubbed at her features, worn away whatever flesh once softened the angles of her jaw and of her cheekbones, revealing a face that is fierce as well as fragile. The fierceness was always there, of course, but now it announces itself. Her good looks are the opposite of the girl-next-door's, the opposite of Carole's.

"William," she says. "You can't . . . you think Jenny is—" She stops. She separates her hands and leaves them open, with their palms up. "I'm not going to say it," she says.

"Is she?"

"Is she what?"

"Were you pregnant when you left me?"

Elizabeth smiles, not warmly, and drops her hands. "I left you the summer we graduated, in August. Forgive me if I don't recall the exact date." Her voice is sharp with sarcasm, enough so that it seems to twang. "I married Paul on September eleventh. Jennifer's birthday is February sixth."

"So you were pregnant when you married Paul."

"Yes."

"And you were pregnant when you left me."

"Possibly."

"So is she mine or Paul's?"

"Well, really, William, who knows? Maybe she's Tom's or Dick's or Harry's. Maybe I was sleeping with any number of people." Elizabeth tosses one arm out as if to include all the men in the tent.

"I'm not judging you," he lies. "I just want to know if you know who her father is."

Elizabeth tips her head up, eyes on the tent canvas overhead.

Veins show green through the white skin of her throat. Oddly sexy, Will thinks, feeling desire awaken. She looks back at him. "Paul is Jennifer's father," she says.

"Because it would be easy enough," he continues as if she hasn't spoken, "to find out if she's Paul's or, well, whoever's."

"I suppose that's true." She gives him a stare of transparently manufactured patience, an expression intended to convey its opposite. Having lost whatever goodwill she once bore him, she's eager to terminate this unfortunate meeting.

"So, have you?" Will presses.

"Have I what?"

"Have you ever had the tests done to see—"

"Look," Elizabeth says. "I'm sorry for what's happened in your life, Will. Truly. I'm sorry for you, sorry for your wife, sorry for your daughter. I admit that I have no idea the pain your family must have suffered. But what you and I had, a college romance, a relationship that's been over and done with for twenty-five years, it can't . . . there's nothing left of that, nothing that could—"

"This isn't about Luke."

"Of course it is."

"No. I just . . . when I saw your page in the reunion book, the bio, the year your daughter was born, I mean, how could the thought not have crossed my mind? How could—"

"You lost a child. Now you want to find one."

"That's a little reductive, wouldn't you say?"

"Absolutely. But can you give me an alternate explana—"

"Elizabeth. You walked out on me. Possibly, you were pregnant with my child. Jennifer was born on—"

"Jenny is twenty-four years old. What's the point of talking about biological paternity now, after another man—Paul—has been her father for all her life?"

"Because. I want to know. I'd think she would, too. And you."

"Seriously?" Elizabeth says. "Surely not seriously."

"Seriously." As he repeats the word, Will realizes that this is in fact what he wants. What he seriously wants. Suddenly, nothing seems more important than learning this one fact. He watches Elizabeth shake her head briskly, as if to dislodge what she's heard.

"But you're . . . you're interested. Is that what you're saying? You're not, you can't be asking me to have this, this thing done."

"Yes, I am."

"No."

"Yes."

"Why!"

"I told you. I want to know."

"*You* do."

"Yes. *I* do."

"But so what? In terms of my life and her life, so what if you want to know? Information like that—it's pointless now. It would only confuse Jenny. Who knows? It could disrupt her education, compromise her understanding of herself. And to what end? To provide you solace? Illusory solace, because it's not going to fix anything, not really."

"But paternity does matter. And I'm not asking for anything to be 'fixed,' whatever that might mean."

"What then?" Elizabeth lays both hands on the table, palms down. She leans forward. "What could possibly be the point?"

"I want to know, that's all. Jennifer doesn't have to. You don't have to. I was thinking . . . well, here's an idea." Will feels his cheeks tingle with surprise at what he's about to say. As if it weren't wine he'd been drinking but a far more potent disinhibitor, a solvent not just for common sense and restraint but whatever keeps a person from voicing everything that pops into his head. "Give me a strand of her hair. You could take it from her brush, tape it to an index card, and mail it to me. Then I could find out. I would know, and that would be it. I wouldn't tell you. I wouldn't tell her. Not unless you specifically asked me to share the results."

Elizabeth stares at him, looking genuinely incredulous, her mouth ajar. "That is very, very perverse," she says.

"What is?"

"Asking me, her mother, to take—steal—her hair."

"It's not stealing."

"It is. It is stealing."

"How can it be stealing if the thing stolen has no value?"

Instead of answering, Elizabeth closes her eyes, long enough that he finds himself studying her face, the mauve skin of her eyelids, her pale mouth and cheeks. She could do with some color, a little lipstick or something, but she's always been too proud to wear makeup. Too assured of herself, one of a minority of those who suffer from high self-esteem.

"It does have value," she says at last, in the measured tone she might use on a retarded adult, someone with the critical capacity of, say, a six-year-old. "Identity has value. Who your parents are is information with value. Obviously it has value to you, enough that you're attempting to convince me to perform an act of, of . . . we won't call it stealing if that offends you. We'll call it, what? How about voyeurism? Like taking a picture of someone who doesn't know you're there, hiding with your camera. You want to peer inside my child, find out what, exactly, she's made of, *who* she's made of, and you have the nerve to ask me—her mother—to be an accessory to this act of voyeurism." Elizabeth is still leaning forward over the table as she speaks, articulating each word with angry precision. "Besides," she says, "why should I believe you when you say you won't do anything with the information? You say you won't tell her, or me, but why should I believe you?"

"I'm trustworthy, Elizabeth. You remember that."

Elizabeth snorts. "Says who?"

"Well, I'm not deceitful. Not like you."

"What!"

"You left me knowing you were pregnant with my child."

"That's . . . that's your fantasy, William Moreland. Your presumption. Not my deceit."

"Prove it."

"Why? Why should I?"

"Because you owe it to me."

Elizabeth gives him a narrow-eyed smile, a look of unambiguous hostility. "I don't owe you anything," she says in a voice that matches the expression.

"Yes. Yes, you do. You do owe me something."

"What?"

"The truth."

"No, I don't." She shakes her head.

The last thing Will wants is to create a scene, and yet he can't stop himself from raising his voice. "You do!" He slaps his hand on the tabletop, not only summoning the attention of those seated nearby but startling himself. What's wrong with him? It's a clinical something, but what? This isn't the only instance, of late, that Will had caught himself struggling to come up with a self-diagnosis. "You do," he says again, less loudly but just as emphatic.

Elizabeth looks at her wristwatch. "I'm going to leave," she says, and she stands.

"Wait," he says. "Just finish this conversation."

"It is finished."

"The honorable thing is to help me find out what I need to know."

"Why? Why do you need to know? What difference will it make? No. Forget that. I know what difference it makes. It's what I said it was. You lost one, you want to find another. But it's too late to find Jennifer, even if she were yours. She's grown up. And"—she points at Will's chest—"can you tell me why is it that men always start talking about honor when they're losing a . . ." She doesn't finish.

"A what?"

"Whatever," she says.

"As a human being, not a friend or an ally but just another human being, don't you think it's fair—I won't say honorable—for me to know if she's my child?"

"She's not. She is not yours. She's hers. She is her own person."

"Fine. Agreed. But she may be a person who is closely, physically, related to me. And one day she may want to know that. For her own well-being she may want genetic information about her father."

Elizabeth shrugs.

"In any case, she doesn't have to know. I want to know, but she wouldn't have to."

"Fuck you," Elizabeth says in a low voice. "Fuck you."

"She wouldn't. Why would she?"

"Because," Elizabeth says. "Because."

"Because why?"

"Do you really not understand that you are being astonishingly stupid?"

"Why would she have to know?"

"Because she's a person, her own person. Not your person or even my person. She belongs to herself."

"Yes, but she, she didn't invent herself, she—"

Twice Elizabeth goes up on the balls of her feet and then slowly lowers her heels, the habit of a woman who's had to come up with strategies to offset the fatigue of standing for much of a workday. Hands on her hips, oblivious to the people, quite a number of them by now, staring and listening, Elizabeth glares at him for what feels like a long time. "I have one thing to say," she says.

"What?"

"You are an excellent example of why it is that people think shrinks are nuts." She snatches her purse, a little black one, from where she's hung it on the chair. She drops it over her head, the long strap crossing her chest like a bandolier, and walks swiftly away, slipping back into the crowd like a new penny dropping into a dark well. He sees a flash of her red hair and then nothing—she's gone.

Will stands, eager to quit the company of people before whom he's behaved so, so . . . how has he behaved?

Badly, that's how. He's behaved badly, stupidly, possibly hurtfully, certainly unadvisedly. He feels the arrival of one of those red-wine headaches, the kind that make it imperative to walk carefully lest he jar it up a notch on the pain scale. And there's no minibar in his room at the hotel, no ten-dollar first-aid kit with Band-Aids, antacids, and two headache pills in a single-serving envelope. If there is a God, the front desk will dispense Advil. If there isn't, he's going to have to walk to a convenience store.

It's just guilt—please make it be a simple case of guilt—but along with the headache, Will feels an increasing sense of dread, or something like it. Foreboding. Not that Elizabeth didn't make it clear that there wasn't a chance she'd respond to his insane (Nuts! Nuts! What the fuck was he thinking!) request. Still, he can't shake the idea that what he's done belongs to the potentially costly rather than simply embarrassing brand of foolishness.

He will write her. An e-mail. He'll say he's sorry, that he's dropped the whole thing.

I t must be the conversation with Elizabeth, Will thinks when he wakes, the room dark, a silver seam of light dividing the curtains. It must be that, because he can't remember the last time he dreamt about Luke.

In the dream, his son had been taken up to heaven.

The boy was white and luminous. He looked as solid as if he were sculpted from marble. Yet light leaked from his body. Every breath streamed and flickered from his lips; every hair on his head was incandescent, a halo of sparks like those thrown off a welder's torch. He was sitting in profile at the top of a fantastically beautiful and treacherous staircase, a staircase chiseled into the face of a cliff formed of glass or of ice, each glistening tread steeper than the one below.

Even from a distance, Will knew that his son was alive, and he began to climb toward him. Having no tools that might on earth prove useful—no pick, crampons, or rope—he willed himself upward, ascending slowly and with an effort that made him gasp and choke. Perhaps he sobbed in his sleep?

The stairs were slippery; they got taller and taller; the uppermost flight almost defeated him.

When he at last reached the top, the light was so intense, he couldn't lift his eyes. It was only by cupping his hands around his face that he could see at all. Even so, the light penetrated, filled his head, informed him that he had reached Luke not because he was strong enough or good enough but because it was inconceivable to him that he would not. Separation from his son was an outcome he was unable to imagine. He had to tell Luke he loved him and not to miss him too badly, not to grieve. He didn't want anything to worry him.

But when at the sound of his voice his son began to incline his face toward him, showing Will its familiar and cherished contours, a face polished and burnished and shining with love—not only his father's but his mother's and his sister's, his grandparents', his uncles', aunts', and cousins', his teachers' and his friends', the love and longing of so many people for this one child—when Luke began to look his way, another boy stopped him, a boy taller and older than his son, a boy Will didn't recognize. The boy put his hand out and touched Luke's cheek to prevent him from turning in the direction of Will's voice.

You must not look at him, the older boy said.

And Luke answered, *But it's my father.*

Luke struggled against the older boy, who Will understood had been assigned to show his son the ropes and prevent such mishaps as the one that had occurred. Because Luke did see Will, just for a moment. Still, it was long enough that his face registered horror.

The older boy said accusingly, *See!*

And Luke asked, *What's happened to him! What's happened to him!*

Nothing, the older boy said. *It's just that that's the way he looks to you now, because he is only mortal.*

Luke sobbed, his face in his hands, and the older boy bent to comfort him.

And Will fell from heaven back to his bed, not down the stairs he ascended, but falling as a man falls from a plane, without a parachute, dropping through space at fatal speed, yet with time to see, and the vision of a god.

At first the city appeared as it would through the window of a jet approaching La Guardia, a tidy arrangement of lives, block after block, with an occasional landmark by which it was possible to orient himself. But then he was closer; he could find his own neighborhood and then his roof among the others on his block, the particular house toward which he was plummeting. What a mess it was in! Cracked façade and derelict rain gutter, two missing storm windows and an inadequately patched leak, broken satellite dish, snarls of TV cable and a useless antenna, its arms askew, like the ribs of a broken, stripped umbrella. Could this really be his house? How was it that Will had allowed it to crumble into such a state of disrepair?

Fast though he fell, Will could see into the rooms of his home as if peering into lidless boxes. There was his wife, and with Carole was Samantha. His mother, his father, and his brother. Neighbors and patients, current acquaintances and people he hadn't seen for decades, even children with whom he'd gone to elementary school—faces he couldn't summon when awake. How small everyone appeared and, like slides from a holiday long past, how nearly transparent. Worse than their smallness was the tiny warmth and throb of them, the insectlike brevity of human life. Unbearable—unspeakable and obscene to be spirit trapped in matter, the bodies we worship and fear, exalt and punish, the flesh that grants every pleasure and ushers in our grief. How awful to be given these sublime and flimsy houses for our souls and then to witness their decay. How monstrous.

The idea of it—flesh—gathered into a fist, or a blow, something that struck him hard on the chest, hard enough that he woke facedown and mouth open, unable even to gasp. As if, in truth, he had fallen from a great height back to earth and hit with a wallop, the dream knocked the breath out of him.

All you, he would have said, were he speaking with a patient about that patient's dream: fragments of you, aspects of you, possible yous, impossible yous, incarnations of you, the you you were, the you you may become, your wishes, your fears, your . . .

But the people he saw as he fell didn't feel like him. And he didn't want the dream Luke to be taken away. He didn't want to have to make his son into, say, a part of himself that looked aghast at another part of him.

What had Luke seen? What did his son see in his face that so frightened and repelled him?

The blue numbers of the digital clock shift from 11:08 to 11:09. He's slept much later than usual, and his body feels stiff and achy, as if in the aftermath of a fever. Will considers the coffeemaker on the dresser, a little basket beside it filled with packets of sugar, artificial sweetener, and nondairy creamer. Eight O' Clock coffee in Christmasy-looking envelopes of tinselly red and green. He tears one open. The ground coffee is packed in a round, white filter, like a doll-sized cushion. He puts this, along with water, into the coffeemaker, and it begins brewing with a congested noise. The contents of the orientation package he picked up the previous day are spread over the table by the window—venue maps and drink vouchers and announcements of added or changed weekend seminars, a seven-page schedule of events that conjures visions of exhausted alumni, some with canes and walkers, lurching from breakfast meetings to round-tables to picnic lunches to step singing (*What is step singing? Could it be singing on steps? Which steps? Surely not those big stone library steps*); memorial services; guided tours of advances in veterinary science; panels; lectures; and God knows what else. The only important thing in the package is the *Class of 1979 25th Reunion Book*. Big black letters on a glossy red cover. Cumbersome and unwieldy as a phone book, it has torn its way out of its shrink-wrap, crumpled and mashed its self-congratulatory cover letter.

Here is the story of your class—your struggles and your triumphs, your journeys from promise into fulfillment . . . Who writes this drivel? Will balls up the letter and drops it in the trash can. Along with all the other members of Cornell's graduating class of 1979, Will had been invited to contribute his dispatch from midlife—*Dear William More-land, We want to hear from you!* And Will had drafted and redrafted and drafted once more his condensed (*No more than 500 words, please!*) autobiography, dividing himself into professional and personal; into husband and father; into brain, body, heart; into year twenty-three, year twenty-four, year twenty-five; into grad student, intern, resident, private practitioner; into citizen and consumer; into into into. There were any number of ways to dismantle himself, but how was he to reassemble his parts into a narrative, a string of words from here to there?

By default, Will became one of the 687 members of his class who didn't contribute to the reunion book, 89 of those having died, 161 "missing," and the rest like himself, he guesses, unable or even unwilling to account for themselves in the form of an essay or a timeline or a résumé illustrated with photographs of children, pets, vacation homes, and fancy cars. Unlike his brother's résumé, rendered in ten-point type to accommodate all his accomplishments, Will's is two lines long: his name followed by what few facts the university has acquired about him since graduation. Ph.D., Psych., Columbia University, 1986; Married to Carole Laski, June 28, 1989; Children, Luke Michael, March 30, 1990; Samantha Jane, October 10, 1996. Member NAAP, APA, NYPA.

So there he is: educated, employed, married, the father of two children. And, like most men within his experience, either as a friend or psychoanalyst, a man transformed by fatherhood as he could not have been by any school or career or woman. Take the arrival of his daughter: wet and naked, arms thrown wide with the shock of her first breath, still tethered to her mother by a glistening rope of blood.

Even now, this moment, how clearly he can see it, the blue and purple vessels bound together in an almost iridescent membrane, slippery and hot—the heat of it against his palm. He cut as directed and then found he didn't want to let it go. Wasn't it a thing too splendid, too holy, even, to burn in a hospital incinerator?

Eight years, almost, since that day, and yet even a familiar glimpse of his daughter can still catch him off guard, grab him with the force of a hand at his throat. The intensity of her concentration when she skips rope, for example, and the way her skinny arms cross at the elbows when she does some of her fancier moves. Through the turning circle she jumps, over and over, the scuff of shoes against pavement alternating with the light slap of the rope. The elastic comes off the end of her moving braid, and her hair, after a few turns of the rope, comes undone and flies up with every jump. She smiles and shows him the completely unexpected beauty of the gap between her teeth. Coming home from work, he finds a smudgy greeting underfoot, chalk hieroglyphs on the sidewalk in front of their house. How many times in a single day can he bear to be shown what is at once too valuable to surrender and guaranteed to be taken? She is flesh of his flesh, a small and perfect creature who is all promise, no regrets or disappointed hopes. He is her father. That her life will have its portion of unhappiness and ill fortune seems impossible, a species of crime, a wrong that must be righted.

Is Carole prey to thoughts like these when she watches their daughter in a school play, when she counts her years in cake candles? Will doesn't think so. The woman he married isn't inclined to melancholy; she neither speculates about what might go wrong nor dwells on what already has. She loves him, even as much as he loves her, Will believes, but she isn't romantic or even sentimental; her boundaries are definite; she has thoughts she will not share and assumes the same is true of him. A blessing, in that certain of his preoccupations are those that might alarm a wife. His sexual fixation, for example, which is beginning to feel too big to keep inside his head. Was there even one woman he encountered the previous evening, one upon whose body he allowed his gaze to linger, without seeing himself—seeing her—well, without seeing what he saw? Even were he to remember one, the act of calling her back before his mind's eye would disqualify her: she wouldn't get away a second time.

He wants to believe that love can't make mistakes, but what he knows is that it's like water, assuming the shape of the vessel, always imperfect, that holds it. He's not a blameless father or a perfect husband, and though he's made a career of listening to other people's problems, he can't always respond with patience and insight. He does bear witness: this is a role as old as childhood, as old as his consciousness of his brother's suffering. He opens old wounds and binds up new ones, strips away defenses, shores up egos. To be paid for the work he craves seems marvelous to Will, a reason to give thanks—but to what, to whom? Because he's also a tortured agnostic, suffering spasms of private, even desolate, self-examination. Alert to coincidence and unanticipated symmetry, to aspects aligning in patterns, almost readable, he sifts, sorts, and turns the pieces, lays them down and picks them up in what amounts to an endless game of mental solitaire, occasionally drawing close to something that comes out neatly and looks like a grand and universal plan, a sequence of details in which, as the saying goes, God resides. Summoned to his door by a pair of canvassing Jehovah's Witnesses, Will not only accepts the literature they press into his hands, he reads it. Accosted on his own corner by a canvassing flock of young Lubavitchers who demand to know if he's a Jew, he stammers in confusion, receiving the question as a challenge to him, him in particular, rather than the proselytizer's customary preface. He's not so much godless as God-bereft.

Armed, of course, with distractions from existential anxiety.

Apart from sex, there's real estate: he's landed. He's even a landlord, if only incidentally and only as a means of managing the debt they carry on their home. A personal trainer who works at a local health club rents the top floor of the brownstone they were lucky enough to buy before the market recovered, a now mostly fixed fixer-upper, with bay windows, an ornate cornice, and a stained-glass skylight: 138 Lincoln Place, in the historic district of Park Slope, named for streets that descend gently from the long, lush meadow and ball fields of Brooklyn's Prospect Park. Both his own and Carole's school loans long behind them, Will is paying down the mortgage, each month chipping away at the principal, reduced now from the $475,000 they borrowed to $280,000. They've lived on Lincoln Place for thirteen years, long enough that the rent for the upstairs apartment at last covers the monthly mortgage, a fact that thrills him, allowing him to tear open statements purely for the pleasure of seeing that his last assault on the principal has been recorded, even if it's no more than a few hundred dollars. It's nothing he could have anticipated, but their mortgage bill has become the single piece of mail to which he always looks forward. Each time he checks the principal, he translates his most recent subtraction from what they owe into its material equivalent: a pocket door, one of the original chandeliers, the parlor's crown molding. Checks made out to him by his patients are welcome, but oddly, they don't inspire the same feeling of accomplishment. Brick by brick, he is making himself and his wife the owners of these four soaring and dignified stories faced with a milk-and-coffee-colored stone that no longer exists in nature, brownstone having been quarried into extinction many years before he was born.

But Will didn't—couldn't—articulate any of what he knows about himself, his essential self, in a five-hundred-word essay. Not any more than did the alumni who submitted their brief, sanitized promos, admitting none of the missteps or misfortunes or unfulfilled longings that might have added texture to their whitewashed autobiographies. No one wrote in to say he'd lusted after his neighbor's wife, and then married her. Or that he'd suffered all his life from gender dysmorphia and was now a woman, no longer Joe but Joanne. Or that, in the wake of her daughter's diagnosis of schizophrenia, she'd fallen into a profound depression that was cured only when she walked out, left her family, abandoned them because, after all, how much was a person expected to endure?

Will scans each page of the reunion book and flips to the next, skimming over advanced degrees and promotions; residencies and relocations; awards and more awards; marriages and births; travel to Turkey, to Tuscany, to Majorca, to Machu Picchu, the Galápagos; marathons, triathlons, thrills of victory, agonies of defeat; PTA committees and car-pool purgatories, these last not so much complaints as advertisements disguised as complaints: *Look at our children; are they not the ultimate wealth and accomplishment?*

Many of the photographs are reproduced from holiday greeting cards, families carefully arranged around sparkling trees, hair combed, eyes bright. Without conscious intent Will finds himself lingering on the faces of those few who admit a family misfortune, looking for evidence of losses on which they don't dwell but make curious asides, rather like sneezing: quick, helpless convulsions that interrupt a text or are bulleted absurdly within the résumé format. These references are abbreviated and in every case weirdly upbeat, their authors clearly having determined to present a hard-won silver lining rather than the lowering black clouds of fate: "Lost my brother to cancer in 1993, and learned a lot about how strong I am!" "Our daughter Kyla, 12, has cystic fibrosis and she is Awesome!!! She is doing Great!!!" "Two brain surgeries, 1999 and 2001—if anyone out

there is suffering unexplained neurological symptoms or has been di-
agnosed with NMH, e-mail me! I love to share!" After each of these
plucky announcements, followed by at least one exclamation point (a
few decorated with little happy-face icons, as well), the afflicted's life
story veers without transition back into the mundane.

This is what Will has come to understand as his problem: transition, an obstacle on the page as in reality, because he insists on it, and
there are unbridgeable divides in a life. Things don't add up; they
don't segue; they follow chronologically, one upon another, without
obeying the more important logic of meaning and sense and, well,
acceptability.

"Not this year," he said to Carole when she asked about their
Christmas card the November after Luke had drowned. For the ten
previous years they'd sent out a photo greeting, not without a guilty,
sheepish irony (at least they'd hoped irony was the evident subtext)
because both he and Carole understood and intended to acknowledge that such cards were inherently obnoxious, even if, to them, irresistible. So they hadn't dressed their best or used a perfect vacation
shot but instead posed in their everyday clothes, each wearing a
goofy Santa hat, Carole with little if any makeup, the kids' hair un-
brushed, Will looking effortfully (and thus less than completely suc-
cessfully) candid. And they trusted that this casual, studiedly
haphazard quality would be taken as an apology for the cards' inher-
ent bragging—*Please forgive us our pride, the pleasure we take in our two
perfect offspring. Overlook, won't you, the vulgarity of our publishing their
inestimable worth. Our living golden calves—how beautiful they are! Our
sacred objects! You must understand that we cannot help ourselves. We can't
not exult.* Will shudders with the recognition, feels the flesh crawl on
his neck. How foolish to flash a target at the jealous gods—to not
merely disregard but show off the chink in their armor. *Aim here!
Here where we presume our divinity and yet are most mortal!*

"No," Will said to Carole. "Not this year."

"Why?" she asked.

"Why!"

"Yes, why?" Carole set her coffee cup on the table and looked at him in that unnerving way she has, her eyes wide with what appeared to be genuine curiosity.

"Because . . . because . . ." He remembers spluttering in outrage, in the face of her calm. "Because one of us is missing! One of us who was in last year's card is gone!"

"Dead," she clarified.

"Dead. Yes. Yes. Dead."

Carole nodded. "Well, everyone knows that. All our friends, they know about Luke. And we could maybe acknowledge him with a, I don't know, something on the—"

"Like what! R.I.P? His initials? His dates? Like a gravestone? A little gravestone in the mail! Happy holidays, and in case you forgot, our son drowned last summer! But don't let that bother you—go ahead and have a wonderful new year!"

"No, that's not—"

"I'm not going to do it."

"You aren't letting me talk. I think we should. For Samantha."

"Why for Sam? It's not as if it's good for her. It's sad for Sam."

"It's sadder if we don't."

So he caved. He tried to arrange his features into an acceptable expression, an expression of what he couldn't say. He's never looked at the photograph Carole picked and had reproduced above their greeting. Two hundred copies. *Peace on Earth*, they probably said, as in years past. Even now he can't figure out what kind of artifact that particular photo greeting might be, or the level—

depth?—of its bad taste. Or maybe it wasn't in bad taste. Maybe it was just what Carole claimed it was: an impossible response to an impossible situation. Apparently she doesn't get stuck there, at Impossibility, the way he does. There is no conceivable transition, so she doesn't insist on it. She's pragmatic in that impressive, fearsome, and always surprising way that women are, the way they preside with equal industry and competence over tea parties and deathbeds.

At home, in the magazine basket by the couch, is *Yoga Journal,* a publication that continues to resurface from under the others because both of them thumb through it, Carole as a disciple, Will as a bystander at once fascinated and incredulous. "A Vedanta Paradigm for Transforming Negative Emotions," the most recent cover promises. Will has reread this article several times, attempting to translate phrases like "the classical citta-vitri-eroding yogic approach" into psychoanalytic terms. But he gets tripped up by discussion of topics like "heart energy" or "the consciousness that has no content" and ends up casting it away in irritation.

He did attempt to recap the last twenty-five years for the reunion book, but he couldn't leave out the drowning, nor could he tell it. What was the previous sentence? What was the one that followed? Will began a letter over and over again, getting no farther than a paragraph before he deleted it from his computer file. According to an online survey, to which 37 percent of the class of 1979 responded, 41 percent of the 37 percent are more spiritual compared with when they graduated, 9 percent less spiritual, 50 percent about the same. Forty-seven percent of them have achieved about what they expected to achieve, 28 percent have exceeded their life expectations, 20 percent are a little disappointed in themselves, and the remaining (unaccounted-for) 5 percent are, he guesses, either apathetic or in despair. Sixty-four percent of them are on their first marriages, 19 percent have remarried, and while the autobiographical dispatches indicate that a few alumni have lost a spouse or a child, no statistical breakdown of tragedies is included in the survey. Nine percent have earned a Ph.D. Forty-one percent choose relaxing vacations, 18 percent cultural, and 25 percent adventurous; 3 percent don't vacation at all. Eighty-two percent claim reading as a favorite pastime, 31 percent "creating," whatever that means.

Perhaps it means gardening or knitting or drawing or, like Sally Henderson, building the world's largest freestanding structure made from discarded plastic bleach containers. Will looks carefully at the picture of Sally standing next to the door of her bleach-bottle tower. Her smile is more rictus than evidence of pride, baring her teeth against a looming threat. Haven't studies of evolution demonstrated that a smile is the pallid descendant of primate rage? A warning of aggression? Will flips quickly through the book, trying to see smiles separate from faces. Are any of these people happy, really? And if they are, how can one tell?

11:57 by the digital clock on the television set. He's missed the ecumenical Sunday service, and if he doesn't hurry, he'll miss brunch in the big tent, as well.

What was it that Luke had seen? he wonders, head bent under the shower's needling spray—the white and shining and exalted Luke of Will's dream. Was it a thing worse than grief, something degenerate and disgraceful, that a child can't allow his father?

The boy in the dream: Will knows he's no more real than a wish, or a fear. And yet, he might ask himself, of what else are we composed?

S o why didn't you stay the whole weekend?" Carole asks him when he comes to bed. "I thought you were looking forward to this thing." The way she says the word *thing* betrays her feelings about reunions, that they are all, without exception, events to be avoided whenever possible.

"I was going to stay. I'd made plans to meet up with a couple of guys, maybe even play some racquetball after the picnic. But, I don't know, after the main attraction, the cocktails and dinner thing on Saturday . . ." Will trails off. He should tell her about running into Elizabeth. Instead, he finds himself talking about Mitch. "After the hundredth person approached to ask me about my famous brother, I got a little tired of the whole thing," he says. Carole makes the face she always does when he mentions his brother, something between a wince and a frown.

"That must have been crummy."

"Well, I should have known. Prepared myself. I guess I was so wrapped up in my own fantasy of his appearing that I didn't consider the more likely scenario."

"Where'd they hold it?" she asks, having apparently decided to move them along to a less loaded bedtime topic. "They'd have to use a basketball court or something for a reception that big."

"There were tents. A separate tent for each class."

"Tents? Ick."

"You don't notice when it's crammed with people. And at least there's fresh air."

"Yes, you do. You do notice." Carole wrinkles her nose. "Even if it doesn't rain, they still have that dank, tenty sort of smell, like old sneakers. Aside from the temporary, makeshift feeling of a Red Cross relief effort."

Will shrugs. "The other thing was, after I'd mingled and reconnected and seen how much hair the men had and if the pretty girls had grown up to be pretty women, and who'd gotten married more than once, or twice, and who'd turned out to be gay, and all the rest of it—after that, it seemed like the next day's activities would be sort of redux. Like those picnics the day after a wedding, when everyone just wants to go home."

"Uh-huh," Carole says, picking up her book. She turns the page.

"So, instead, I hung out at the hotel and watched triple-X movies on pay-per-view."

"Yeah?" she says. Will pulls the book from her hands. "Hey! What are you doing!"

"You're not listening to me."

"Yes, I am."

"What did I say, then?"

"That you mingled and it was . . . it was like a picnic."

"No. I said I left and watched triple-X movies at the hotel."

She looks at him. "You did?"

"No! I just said that to see if you were paying attention."

"I'm sorry, Will," she says, and she moves closer to him. "I know a way back into your good graces."

"Do you? How?"

Carole slides one hand under the waistband of his pajama bottoms.

"Yeah?"

"Yeah. But first give me back my book."

"You don't need it. Not now."

"I want to mark my place." She pulls her hand out of his pants, lets the elastic go with a little snap, but instead of returning the book, Will lifts it high out of her reach. "Give it," she says, "or I'm down-grading you to a hand job."

"What? No way!"

Carole makes a grab for the paperback, and Will rolls out from under her, keeping it out of reach. He opens to a random page, reads aloud in a voice of breathless suspense.

"'Glatman jerked the ligature around Christine Rohas's slender neck. His knee in the small of her back, he pinned her to the ground, facedown in a field where, only hours before, the local peewee championship was played. Swiftly, he bound her ankles and through the loops threaded the end of the rope trailing from her neck. One brutal tug, and . . .'" Will closes the paperback to consider its lurid cover, which promises *sixteen pages of shocking photos!* "I really don't see how this can compare to my report of who from the class of 'seventy-nine went bald and who didn't." Carole lunges, and the fitted bottom sheet springs off one and then another mattress corner as she tries to wrestle his arm down.

"Now, how is it that you can square something like this with higher consciousness and feminism and yoga and all that?" he asks, holding the book far above her head. Carole gets up on her knees, but as soon as she pries one hand off the cover, the other has it fast.

"I don't," she says.

"Stop it. You can't pull hairs out of my arm."

"Why not?" Accidentally, Carole kicks the bedside table, toppling a stack of exemplary reading material: professional journals, novels chosen by her Thursday book group, *New Yorker*s of varying vintage, arts and education sections pulled and saved from the *Times*, all lying untouched. The books she actually reads, with titles like *Hillside Stranglers*, *The Greenriver Killer*, *Beauty Queen Slasher*, she keeps hidden from view, on the top shelf of her closet—enough true crime to fill two banker's boxes with the rape and murder, or murder and then rape, of young women—cheap paperbacks whose covers bear snapshots of the victims taken in happier times, on holidays and at high school graduations, mementoes from a family album. "Basically, this is porn," Will says, paging through the photo insert.

"Okay, it's porn."

"Otherwise, why hide it?"

"Because it's not for children, obviously. It's not for Sam to see."

"Meaning unsavory. Subject to parental censorship."

"Yes. I admit everything. Now give it."

"Lowbrow. Do you admit to lowbrow?"

"Yes."

"You'd die of embarrassment if your book group caught you?"

"I don't know that I'd die."

"You wouldn't like it."

"I wouldn't like it. Let go, Will, you're tearing the cover."

He lets her have it. Lying on his side, he props his head on one elbow. "They don't turn you on, do they?" he says.

"Sexually, you mean?" Carole looks at him, raises an eyebrow.

"Sure. You know, sex so radically sexy it's fatal."

She shakes her head. "Disappointed?"

"A little. What about recipes? I thought women liked to read recipes."

"Boring."

"Romances?"

Carole turns out the light. "Don't you think I deserve a secret vice?" she says, sliding her hand under his T-shirt and stroking his chest. "A teeny-weeny vice that doesn't hurt anyone?"

"No."

She tugs on the waistband of his pajama bottoms, and Will lifts up, off the bed, slides them down. "I want you to have big fat vices. Give in to your basest impulses."

"Do you?" She pulls her nightgown over her head. "What do you imagine those impulses might be?"

"Hard to say." Will shudders as her mouth touches him. The hairs on his arms and thighs lift his skin into gooseflesh at the wet heat of it, that shock of pleasure that never wears off. "Probably nymphomaniacal."

"Huh," she says, substituting hand for mouth. "You don't think that secretly I might be a compulsive shopper? Or, um . . . let's see, a gambler? A glutton maybe?"

"No. Not for food, anyway."

"Why not?"

"I can tell that you're a sex addict," he says, "by the way you can't let more than a few seconds go by without taking me in your mouth again." With his hand on the back of her neck, Will guides his wife's head back to where he wants it.

W ill waits for his father at Molyvos, a Greek restaurant in midtown with a tiled floor and walls the color of terra-cotta. It's not the quietest place, but the lunchtime crowd has started to thin, and the layout makes for a lot of small corner tables, a sense of privacy if not calm. Will prefers to have his back to the wall, but he takes the chair and saves the banquette for his father, who gives his shoulder a hello squeeze before he slides in.

"So," he says. "How's Carole? Sam?"

"They're good. Sam's loving this crazy tai kwon do class we put her in. Spends hours bowing to herself in the mirror. Carole's working too many hours—big surprise. There's some sort of grievance developing between the union and the district, but her position probably won't be affected by whatever changes are made. If any changes are made."

"So she did sign the contract?"

Will nods. In addition to her private practice, Carole has recently taken a job with District 15, screening children for speech disorders. Four mornings a week, she administers diagnostic tests at either P.S. 321 or P.S. 282 in Park Slope, or at P.S. 8, a progressive elementary school in Brooklyn Heights. No retirement package, but benefits that include health insurance at a rate much more affordable than what he can get through NAAP.

Will waves the waiter away. "We need a few minutes," he says. He points at a book in his father's upper-left-hand pocket. "What's that?"

His father pulls out a paperback copy of *Frankenstein* and asks Will if he's read it.

"A long time ago."

His father frowns. "I wasn't expecting it to be so sad," he says, thumbing through the pages. "I'd stop, but you know how I am. Can't walk out of a bad movie. Can't cancel a trip to the beach because rain's forecast."

"Where are you?" Will asks him when he doesn't look up from the book. "What part?"

The two of them meet once a month, just to see each other, keep up. Sometimes they talk about books they've discovered, movies they've seen, and Will is often surprised by his father's choice of reading material. Last month it was *Zen and the Art of Motorcycle Maintenance.*

"Just finished volume two," his father says, and closes the book. "The monster has killed Frankenstein's son. And he's requested a female companion as hideous and deformed as himself, so that he can make love to a creature that won't turn away from him in revulsion." Will's father closes his eyes for a moment. "Isn't it curious that such a tragic figure would have become, a hundred years later, a kind of joke? A hulking, green bungler with big boots and bolts in his neck. A figure of derision. Not capable of an act as focused as a hateful, vengeful murder."

"Why are you reading it?"

He shrugs. "I don't know. I was in the bookstore, looking through the classics because, you know, I skipped so many. I picked it up, put it back on the shelf, ended up coming back to it when nothing else caught my eye. Something about the cover, must have been."

He holds it up, but the picture's too small for Will to see clearly from across the table, and his father hands it to him. It's a reproduction of a painting—six people gathered around a table and above them, on a pedestal, a white bird trapped inside a glass globe. Will turns the book over to read the fine print on the back cover. "A detail from 'An Experiment on a Bird in the Air Pump,' a painting in the National Gallery," he tells his father. No date is given for the work, and Will has never heard of the artist, Joseph Wright. The bird is caught in an unnatural position, one wing extended, perhaps broken, and a tube attaches the sealed glass globe to a sinister-looking apparatus. The whole scene is lit dramatically so that a flood of yellow light picks out certain details and leaves others in darkness, as in a crucifixion by Caravaggio, for example.

"Doves usually represent the holy spirit, don't they?" Will asks his father.

"Guess so," he says. "Distressing, seeing an animal trapped like that." The waiter returns and Will's father points to a line on the menu. Will leans forward, trying to see what he's chosen.

"What are you getting?" he asks him.

"Dolmades?"—*dole maids*—"Is that how you say it?"

Will shrugs. "Grape leaves," he says. "With rice inside and something else, I'm not sure what."

Across the table, his father is patting the many pockets of his sportsman's vest as if to remind himself of their contents, a gesture that has become habitual, even compulsive. Once he'd sold his veterinary practice and discarded his lab coats, he created what is in effect a new uniform: the khaki vest with numerous pockets, all of which he fills; wide-wale, navy blue corduroy trousers; and a fishing hat that looks like an upside-down flowerpot. The hat might be funny on another man—on anyone but his father—and Will has himself to blame for the vest. After he complained to his mother that he and Carole

were receiving too many of what they'd begun to refer to as his father's "booty calls," his mother bought the vest so his father wouldn't
have to carry his cell phone in the back pocket of his trousers, into
which he'd jam the thing and then sit on it while driving, inadvertently putting pressure on whatever button he'd programmed to
speed-dial Will's home number. Whoever picked up would hear the
thrum and whoosh of highway travel punctuated by random throat
clearings and sometimes the strains of whatever song was playing on
the local oldies station. "Dad!" Will would yell. "DAD!" But his father never heard the tiny voice coming out from underneath him,
and once Will had answered the phone, he found it difficult to hang
up and sever the connection. Though his father was oblivious to his
phantom presence in the car—or perhaps because he was oblivious—
there was an unexpected intimacy in having been summoned to ride
along with him, invisible and undetected, returned to his ten-year-
old self, happy to be with his father, no matter how workaday the er-
rand.

"So," Will says to him after the waiter has left, "I talked with
Mom."

"Oh," his father says. "And?"

"She told me it's that woman you met at the gallery. The one who
bought all those prints."

"Yup."

"You're living with her?" Will asks.

"I like the city."

"I didn't ask you how you felt about New York. That's not—"

His father smiles. "I know." Silver hair and laugh lines have made
Will's father improbably handsome, more so than either of his much
younger sons, more than when he himself was younger and women
already found him irresistible, so that they'd linger in the exam room,
schedule appointments for healthy animals, drop by the clinic with

questions about dewclaws or ear mites or housebreaking, whatever they could think of. Will remembers his mother being good-humored about this, but then, his father hadn't given her reason to be jealous, not back then. Or at least he hadn't as far as Will knew.

His father plays with a rubber band on his wrist. "I spend a few nights in town, then go back home."

"What about Mom?"

"She's busy enough that she doesn't seem to take much note of where I am."

"Is that what this is about? You feel like she's not paying attention to you?"

"She's not. But that's not what this is about." The waiter sets their plates before them, and his father picks up his fork. "Your mother and I have been married for nearly fifty years," he says. "You don't think we've paid attention to each other the whole time, do you?"

"I guess I'm just trying to figure this out—what it means."

"Does it have to mean something? I like spending a few nights a week in the city. I like spending time with Lottie."

"Lottie?"

"Charlotte."

"She's good company?" Will says. "What do you talk about?"

"Nothing much. We rent movies. DVDs. She has a good setup. Big screen. Like a little theater, almost."

"She's rich, Dad," Will says. His father nods, chews. "But that can't be—" Will is suddenly aware that he's pinching the skin over his Adam's apple, pulling at it absentmindedly as he does sometimes while concentrating, especially on something that bothers him. "There must be something else," he says.

His father looks at him, raises his eyebrows. "There is."

"Oh, God," Will says. "Don't tell me this is about sex."

"I didn't introduce the topic."

"It is about sex?"

"Will," his father says. He puts his knife and fork down and leans forward over his plate. "I take it your mother told you I was having an affair. Doesn't that imply that it's about sex?"

"But . . ." *You're seventy-four,* he was going to say, his mind already jumping to Viagra, and then to one of his patients, only two years older than Will, who uses a cocktail of Viagra and Cialis, each prescribed by a different physician, neither of whom knows about the other or that the man doesn't even have a problem with sexual performance. "My happiness," the patient had said when Will challenged him, "is predicated on my getting this reward. The only time I feel really good, really alive, is when I'm getting laid. And everything I do, all the effort I put into my career, my wife, my kids—it's all about earning my right to have relations with as many ladies as possible."

"As many as possible," Will repeated. The man nodded.

"I feel okay about that," the man said. "I work hard. I couldn't work any harder. I feel I'm entitled." He looked at Will. "Who's getting hurt?" he demanded, and then he answered himself. "No one, that's who."

Across the table, Will's father is smiling. "Will," he says, "I'm not asking for your permission, or your advice, or congratulations. Let's talk about something else. Let's talk about you. How's work?"

Will shakes his head. "I have a problem," he says.

"Yeah? What sort?"

"I'm not sure. I'm trying to figure it out." His father tilts his head to one side, frowns. *Come on,* the expression says, *get to the point.* Will draws a deep breath. "For the past month or so, every time I'm in session with a female patient, I end up, I don't know, having this, uh, physical response to her. It's weird. Nothing like this has ever happened to me before."

"Physical meaning sexual?" his father asks, and Will nods.

"As if she were the most desirable woman on earth, and I the most sexually starved man. Makes no difference what she looks like."

"Huh," his father says. "So what do you do?"

"What do I do? Nothing, of course."

"Not with your patient. I mean, what do you do about dealing with the problem?"

"Check in with Daniel, I guess. I've made the appointment."

"Daniel, your what's it called, trainer?"

"Training analyst," Will says. "Basically, the mandate is that any time an analyst experiences feelings that are inappropriate or that might compromise the relationship between him and a patient, he goes back to his own analyst. Whoever it is he sees when a situation like that comes up."

"Countertransference," his father says, nodding.

"Right. But countertransference is a neutral term. It isn't necessarily wrong or even untherapeutic. Just sometimes."

"You see Mitch?" Will asks to change the topic. His father wrinkles his forehead in an expression of something that looks like apprehension. "On TV," Will clarifies, and his father shakes his head.

"When was this?"

"Sunday last. CNN, I think. Some filler show called *People in the News*."

"Oh?" his father says.

Will nods, watching his expression. "Same old, same old." His father doesn't answer, and Will frowns at him. "It still bugs me, you know it does, his turning his back on all of us. I can't square it. Coming after . . . after he was . . . well, after that toast at the rehearsal dinner."

His father waves a hand through the air. "Let it go," he says, as he does whenever Will drags Mitch into their conversations. *Let it go. Let him go. Give it a rest. Do yourself a favor: let it go.* But how?

Will doesn't say anything, remembering his brother the summer they were at camp together in the Adirondacks, both of them thirteen, an age he associates primarily with the onslaught of wet dreams. He sees Mitch's long body moving underwater, white, ghostly, aimed toward the dock where Will was standing, his face breaking through the surface. He came up out of the water and onto the dock in one motion, already more graceful and at ease in water than on land. It was an all-boys camp they attended that summer, and some of the campers teased Mitch about his birthmark, a port-wine stain that colored more than half of his face purple, but it had been Will whom this angered. Mitch was stung, he must have been, but whatever pain he felt in the moment seemed to fade. Or rather, Mitch faded, he became increasingly vague and distant—in Will's memory it's as if he is out of focus, an outline blurring into the background—while Will seethed with rage he couldn't control. Like two people long married, he and Mitch had developed a tacit, if not unconscious, symbiosis, one in which Will bore their humiliation, both the shame of his twin's disfigurement as well as the imperative to respond to insult. For his part, Mitch represented their capacity for patience and long-sufferingness. Superficially, he did.

That summer, Will got into fights on his brother's behalf and, after bloodying a boy's nose, was given formal warning by the camp director. A report of his misconduct was sent home to their parents, and in reparation for the nose, he'd been denied an afternoon of tubing on the river, instructed to spend those hours composing a letter of apology to the owner of the nose and another letter to the nose's mother and father. As he remembers it, he had to write about a dozen drafts of each before he was able to purge the letters of recriminations against the boy he'd punched, and it required an extraordinary act of will to actually form the word *sorry*. Then, not an hour after he'd presented the letters to the director, he overheard a kid call Mitch an ugly douche bag and, before he knew what he was doing, had attacked him. The camp director called their parents to ask that they pick Will up; he was expelled.

Mitch was encouraged to stay, but the twins left together, and though there was little discussion of what had happened, it was that summer, before eighth grade, that Will and Mitch and their parents became aware of what should have been apparent for some time: his and Mitch's mutual, even symbiotic, maladjustment. Because Mitch had to bear the birthmark physically, Will had assigned himself its psychic burden.

"Hey," his father says, "where'd you go?"

"Nowhere. Actually, I was thinking about that summer I got kicked out of camp."

"What about it?"

"I don't know. I guess it was the beginning of my being aware that things between Mitch and me were pretty seriously screwed up. That I didn't respond to people on my own terms, or for my own sake, because I'd fallen into the habit of empathizing with Mitch. As if nothing were happening to me, not really, or not independently. I know, I know," he says, seeing his father's expression. "You've heard this before. And what's the use in going back over it? I just wish the two of us had talked more. Or at all."

His father is still shaking his head, as if the very fact of his other son is baffling, unknowable. "I guess nothing else gives him what he gets from swimming," he says. It's not unusual for Will's father to make non sequiturs, voicing only the last in a series of thoughts.

"What's that?" Will asks.

"I don't know. Beauty, maybe. Excitement. Simultaneous fulfillment of his life and his death wishes." Will says nothing. His father pulls a credit card from his wallet. "This one's mine," he says, and he lays the card on the check, motioning to the waiter. "What's the word for the death wish? *Thanatos? Eros* and *thanatos?* Life and death?"

Will nods. "What else are you reading, Dad? *Frankenstein* with a little Freud on the side? A dash of Ferenczi?"

His father smiles as he signs the receipt and slides out from the banquette; he stands and his napkin falls from his lap onto the floor. Will picks it up and lays it on the table. He looks at his watch. "You want to walk a little ways? I'm running early."

"Sure. Samantha still seeing that woman?" his father asks, alluding to Laura, the child psychologist.

"No, no. She hasn't gone since last spring."

"Yeah? That's good, no?"

"I think so. It's hard to say with kids. It's, not as if Luke's death won't stay with her for all her life. Inform who she becomes. But for all that, she doesn't appear unhappy. I'm always looking for symptoms, of course, signs of depression, anxiety, but she seems okay. Genuinely okay. I see her in the school yard. She skips, giggles, plays with the other little girls. She's the president of their jump-rope club. In two years she's going to set a world record, she says, but she doesn't have to start practicing until she turns nine."

"Sounds normal to me," his father says.

Will points to *Frankenstein.* His father is patting the book through his pocket. "Is this classics thing an attempt to suck up some culture so you have something to talk about with, with—what's-her-name, Carla?"

His father grins at him. "Charlotte," he says, "and we don't need things to talk about."

"Nothing?"

"Not much."

They stand just inside the restaurant door, looking out at the people on the sidewalk, the taxis, the buildings that look like walls of glass. A thick fog swirls down the avenue. "It's very strange," Will's father says, "having sex with someone other than your mother. I hadn't done that in, well, decades."

"Forty-nine years," Will says. "Almost fifty. A half-century. Golden anniversary coming up."

His father smiles his disarming smile. "I'm not sure if the sex is better," he says. "Maybe it's just different. One thing—it's reacquainted me with my body, sort of yanked me back into it, like I haven't been for as long as I can remember. Started trimming my toenails with attention. Flossing my teeth. Upgraded my underwear."

"How's Mom feel about it?"

"You know, Will, she's very happy being a businesswoman. She likes it a great deal."

"So much so that she doesn't care if you're cheating on her?"

After Will's father sold his veterinary practice, and perhaps in response to his having embarked on a new, solitary career as a photographer rather than settling into leisure with her, Will's mother transformed herself into a dervish of housework, not so much a woman as one of those tornadoes that blew out of a bottle of, what cleanser was it? Mr. Clean?—something advertised in the late sixties, when he and Mitch came home from school on winter afternoons and watched too much television. Not that she'd been uninterested in hygiene before, but her commitment had ebbed as much as it flowed, never reaching an obsessive standard. But, having scrubbed their house in Ravena until there was no carpet left to pull up, no floor to strip or tub to scour or window to wash, she turned her attention to other people's homes, creating a business, overnight it seemed.

Heaven Help You is the name of Will's mother's cleaning service; her business card includes a graphic of an antic mop wearing a halo. She'd started out with two young women and now employs twelve, sending them forth in teams of three, charging one hundred dollars an hour and clearing 20 percent of the gross. Will went back to his hometown some months after she'd established herself, and the whole place looked cleaner to him. As if his mother's frenzy for order and cleanliness had penetrated as far as the town council, there were new litter barrels on the corners, and a shining yellow street cleaner came by, spraying water on his bumper as it turned its massive brushes against the curb.

As they exit the restaurant, Will's father reaches out and touches him gently on the chest. "Cheating implies that I'm being dishonest. I'm not. I asked her permission."

"You're kidding." They walk out into air heavy with moisture.

"No, I'm not. I'm not kidding."

"I guess I missed that part."

"Oh? What part did she tell you?"

"I don't know. How many are there?"

Will's father doesn't answer this.

"I called to talk to you," Will says. "She gave me a number in Manhattan, and when I asked whose it was, she said, 'Your father's girlfriend's.'"

"Huh."

"I tried to get her to talk to me, but no dice."

"She thinks you blow things out of proportion."

"So she told you it was fine with her if you went ahead and had an affair?"

"What she said was she trusted me to determine how important it was for me to do this. And that if I decided I really did need to, then she accepted that."

"*Need* to?" Will asks.

"Okay—want to."

"And is there parity? If Mom decides she needs or wants to explore sex with another man, is that all right with you?"

"Of course. I'm not a hypocrite." Will's father stops walking and looks up at the slice of sky over the avenue, a luminous gray band. Already his vest is covered with a layer of fine droplets. "I don't think she's all that interested, though."

"That's lucky." Will manages to say this without sounding peevish. It must be that he's feeling guilty for having facilitated his father's entry into the art world, and thus his arrival at infidelity to his mother.

After a period of trial and error that he now calls his apprenticeship, Will's father had come to Brooklyn with a shirt box filled with what he judged were the best among his photographs, and asked Will if they could go together to a gallery in Manhattan.

"I don't think it works that way, Dad," Will told him, not wanting any part in what he was sure would prove a disappointment.

"Well, how does it?"

"You can't just walk in off the street. I'm sure you need an introduction or something, a—"

"Maybe," his father said, and he smiled. What did he know? the smile said. He was a retired veterinarian. But Will lived in the city. He must know someone, didn't he?

Yes, actually, the mother of a friend of Luke's, yet another someone eager to inoculate herself against whatever it was that had fallen upon Will and his family. She'd gladly do a favor—*Anything! Just ask!*—to address the difference between them, the fact that her child was living and his was not. An editor at *Art News*, she knew a number of gallery representatives, and in a gesture akin to throwing salt over her shoulder, she took the box of prints into her clean hands. Will could assure his father, she told him, that she would be responsible for their handling.

To Will's astonishment, within a few months, his father's work was picked up by a small gallery on Greene Street, his photographs mounted, framed, and hung on a freshly painted wall, celebrated with an opening announced on creamy, deckle-edged invitations and catered by attractive, hip young men and women who carried trays crowded with glasses of champagne, caviar rolled into tiny blini, and slices of honeydew wrapped in prosciutto sliced so thin it was almost invisible.

Henry Moreland was an instant and happy success, his work favorably mentioned in *Art News* and *Photography*, his show recommended by *Time Out*, embraced not just because he was old but because he was a retired animal doctor. Having been a humble sort of savior, a man who'd never cultivated connections in the sniping New York art world, never sucked up to anyone or done anything to invite spite, Will's father was forgiven his talent. Gracious at the opening, he introduced Will's mother—wearing a new dress and salon-styled hair—to people she would never see again, among them the woman with whom he'd embark on an affair. Will and Carole had watched all this from where they stood, on the party's periphery, grateful to have Samantha between them, the necessity of answering her questions, of collecting her half-eaten hors d'oeuvres and finding her a cup of water that didn't sparkle, of wiping up her spills and asking her again to please not point, not even at people whose clothes were designed to awe and confound.

The crowd of flushed celebrants; the trays of filled champagne flutes; the indecipherable praise; the little cards that read "Price available upon request": none of this was what Will's father had imagined for his old age. But, on the other hand, as his modest smile implied, it wasn't unwelcome.

"Dad?" Will says now, as they stop for a red light, "when you're working, taking a picture or printing it, do you ever feel something's being revealed to you? That your consciousness is heightened—augmented, maybe—by a force outside of your own intellect? That you understand something you hadn't before?"

His father looks at him. "I don't know. I can't tell what you're talking about. Do you mean something to do with God?"

"It wouldn't have to be. It could, but it wouldn't have to."

They walk in silence for a block, then cross Forty-seventh Street. Ahead are the bright lights of Times Square, mesmerizing, each neon shape bleeding into the fog and creating its own aura of color. So many more giant screens than there were even a few years ago, it seems to Will. On the side of one building a series of portraits appear, each for a second or two. He watches to see what the monumental faces are selling. Insurance of some kind, life insurance, or health. Or maybe it's financial planning, mutual funds. Beyond them, he can just make out the shadowy outline of 1 Times Square, the building on top of which the glittering New Year's Eve ball slides down a flagpole, its audience, five hundred thousand strong, counting down the seconds to their lists of resolutions, or at least to clean slates. Will has never understood why a giant disco ball is the country's chosen symbol of time moving forward, and shouldn't the big orb go up rather than down? So un-American to descend. America was all about upswings and bootstraps and mind-over-matter, a confidence so profound—or was it blind?—it ensured the country would always be out of step with the rest of the world.

"Are you talking about inspiration?" his father asks. "Whether it comes from within a person or from without?"

"I don't know. What's inspiration?"

His father frowns thoughtfully, says nothing.

The photographs his father takes mystify Will. Whenever he visits, he looks at his father's most recent work, going slowly through the images, many of which he can place in the town where he grew up: benches he's sat on, signposts he's swung from, mailboxes and sewer covers and barber poles. But no sculptures or fountains or fancy weather vanes; his father prefers the artless and unassuming among possible subjects, and points his camera at things that stay put. There are no people and no animals, not even trees that aren't incidental, blurred background. Only objects, humble objects strangely transformed by his father's vision. It must be the light, Will has decided, the angle of the sun, the time of day, perhaps a filter that removes light waves of a particular length. What else could elevate a seemingly inventory art into a catalog of yearning? Even a lamppost looks as if, unfulfilled by life as a lamppost, it's on the brink of evolving into something else, something truer and brighter and realer. By virtue of a silent, invisible intent, it seems to shimmer, caught just at that moment before it disappears, changes, becomes another thing, or a nonthing—animate, potent, and unexpected.

Or maybe it isn't a function of light; maybe it's just projection. Maybe what Will sees is his own need to believe in a father who has the ability to alter the world around himself, or, at the least, to show Will what a new, illuminated world might look like.

"Well," his father says, "aside from painting and music and what have you, aren't you asking the old God question? Whether or not God exists outside of faith? Independent of our faith?"

Will looks at him. "Weird how as you get older you find yourself less and less certain of anything."

"Just wait," his father says. "You have no idea."

"Mom believes in God, doesn't she?"

His father shakes his head. "That's a very private question," he says. "I don't think I've ever asked her directly."

"Carole does. Or maybe she doesn't. She seems at peace with life, with herself. Not like me. I think she might be what they used to call a secular humanist. Brimming over with unaccountable optimism.

Even after Luke. Even now, when every day brings more evidence of how many messes we've made that we can't undo. Environmental damage. Terrorism."

His father nods slowly. "Sometimes," he says, as he steps onto the curb, "when I print a picture, I see that I've photographed what I didn't know was there. Whatever it is, it's something I looked at without seeing. So I'm surprised, I feel something's been given to me. But by whom? What?" He looks at Will. "There's a quote I came across. I can't get it out of my head. 'The unconscious is God's country.'" He folds his arms over his chest, frowning. "That's the reason I've been reading up on it—Freud, Jung. What do you make of it?"

"What's the context?" Will asks. "Who said it?"

His father makes a swatting gesture. "I can't remember. What I want to know is, is it true? Do you, as a psychoanalyst, someone who's always mucking about in there, think it's true?"

Will frowns. "Well, the unconscious would be the place from which irrational fears and hopes, dreams—"

His father interrupts. "Whoever it was, that's not what they were talking about."

"You didn't let me finish."

"I know where you're going, and it's a little more mysterious than that."

"No, you didn't let me finish."

"All right. I'm listening."

"Okay. This is the only way I can answer. I've thought about Luke's continued existence. I don't mean my wish that he live on, but the conflict—the discontinuity—between his presence within me and his absence in the world. I've ascribed that, that disparity to the unconscious. My unconscious. I know that Luke's . . ." Will stops, unable, for a moment, to speak. When he does, the first few words come out choked. "I know he's dead," he says, reaching for his father's arm.

"But only when I'm awake, conscious. In my unconscious, Luke lives. The realness of him in my dreams is, is so . . . I wake up, and the bed, the floor, my wife, my own hand—nothing has the . . . the reality, the incandescent life of the child in my dreams. My unconscious.

"So," Will says, "maybe that's an example of the unconscious being God's country. A place of life after death. Of resurrection. Reunion with those who die before us."

His father nods, looking up. "Heaven," he says. "Just as it's always been promised."

T he responsible thing to do—he tells himself every day—would be to take a leave of absence.

Instead, Will has done the opposite. As if to foreclose opportunities for reflection, the danger of too much time spent exploring his own psyche, he's expanded his caseload to make a total of nineteen weekly patients as well as one daily and five thrice-weekly analysands to whom he listens and comments. Comments appropriately, despite whatever alarming, inappropriate sexual scenario is unspooling in his head. Even comments wisely, if he is to believe one fervent letter of thanks.

Denial? Defiance? The exhausting prospect of having to refer all his patients to other therapists, either temporarily, meaning he could look forward to returning to all the compounded distrust and anger his abandonment inspired, or permanently, meaning he'd have to start over and build a new practice from scratch? No matter the reason—and perhaps it's as simple as the inability to imagine himself not working—Will continues on as he has been. "To hell in a hand-basket" is the phrase that pops into his head, one of his mother's tidy dismissals, an announcement that she's "washing her hands" (there's another) of whatever mess it is.

He knows its cause, or at least what he assumes has forced the development of his own lust into a drive he can no longer govern or contain, a drive that has pushed him beyond the boundary of what he used to recognize as himself. He can even guess, within a few days, the night of this catalyst's arrival. Carole was sitting across from him at the dining room table, dinner long over, Samantha asleep, plates stacked in the sink. He was looking at the table's surface, watching the arc of moisture left by the sponge as it evaporated, disappeared, looking at this rather than at his wife's face when he asked her, "Are you *tired*?" Because it was at this moment that he decided it was time: a decent interval had passed. Or if not decent, then bearable. What exactly was the sexual etiquette of mourning? All he knew was he'd waited as long as he could, hating himself for the calculation and for possessing desire that was unkillable, and therefore indecent.

Hesitant, afraid of causing insult, he didn't ask the literal question but couched it as one of their oblique invitations for intercourse, that is, Are you *too* tired?

Carole looked at him. "All right," she said, taking no trouble to conceal that this would be what they call a mercy fuck, an indulgence of his need, a gift she could afford to give him.

No, not afford. *Afford* belonged to the past, before the accident, when minor questions seemed to have answers of consequence. *What restaurant? Which movie? Shower or bath? A walk to the park? Window-shopping along the avenue? White wine? Red?* That it had once been worth considering such choices seemed marvelous, a matter over which to marvel. "All right," Carole said, and he guessed this was because it didn't matter to her what they did or didn't do. What could be given to her? What could be taken away? Nothing that would return them to the consideration of minutiae.

But they hadn't made love since the morning before Luke drowned, and Will felt an awkward and uncomfortable something growing between them, a film of alienation that was almost tissuelike, thickening with every passing hour, acquiring that much more substance. Soon this membrane would be opaque; soon he wouldn't be able to see beyond it to his wife on the other side. He went up the stairs behind her, eye level with the back of her tanned thighs, feeling his gratitude. She would open herself to him. He could follow his body and disappear into hers. For a little while he could.

Carole undressed. She flipped back the covers and lay down without turning off the light. "Did you want it on?" he asked, because she didn't usually.

"If you do." She turned onto her side to face the window, and Will couldn't see her expression. He bent down to pull off his socks and got into bed carefully so that it didn't jounce or creak, drew toward her to embrace her from behind. She turned onto her stomach.

"Do you want to do it that way?" he asked, after a silence.

"Yes."

"You don't want to start the other way?"

"Not really."

So he entered his wife from the back, which he liked—he liked it just as well as any other way, better sometimes—and when he asked, a few minutes later, "Do you want to turn over?" again Carole said she didn't.

She was on her hands and her knees, and he bent over her damp back, reaching to touch her. But he'd barely brushed her pubic hair when she moved his hand. "No?" he said, and she shook her head. He stopped moving; immediately his erection started to ebb inside her.

"Well, will . . . will you do it?" he asked, and she touched herself with her own hand. Obediently, she worked her way toward orgasm.

Carole could deny it, but Will understood the meaning of her silent compliance. It was a judgment against him. Against any organism so primitive that it could take comfort in flesh, against a bereaved father who chose this brief oblivion, who allowed himself a comfort he didn't deserve.

Except *deserve* was his language, not hers. So perhaps she was right: he was unfair, he projected his disgust onto her, he craved punishment as much as he did sex and cleverly manipulated her into a vessel for both. He'd scripted her as his monolithic mother, was that it? The great force who gave and who withheld, who soothed even as she condemned. And Carole was indulgent enough to act this out.

"Oh God, Will! Shut up! Won't you please, please just stop?" she says when he drags her down after him into one of his psychoanalytic rabbit holes, refusing to plummet with him through his bottomless, convulsive guilt.

Whatever it means, it did begin that August evening, their new one-position sex life, unvarying to the point of ritual. Ritual and seemingly irrevocable, as conclusive as a burned bridge, Luke's death the obvious divide. Did this have to be an issue? Did he have to make it into an issue? Were he to accept without deconstructing the shift, he might grow used to it, complacent even. Many husbands—he can think of several—would celebrate a wife who took care of her own pleasure and left him to concentrate on his. But increasingly, Will found this hard, very hard. And the fact that she still went down on him but wouldn't let him touch her, neither with finger nor tongue— so that there could be no parity (not that anyone was measuring, except of course they were, people always did measure everything, especially love and acts of love)—and the disparity made it, well, it's hard to say it made anything worse, in that whatever might include blow jobs can't be *worse*, but it did make it more pointed: their having lost their balance.

That first night—a real first night in that losing Luke had changed them, not returning them to virginity but bringing them to a different state of clumsy self-consciousness and second-guessed gestures, of lacking the skills needed to make it turn out right, the fear of wounding or offending or simply asking too much of the flesh: What could it do? How far away could it take them? How much comfort could it hold?—after Will came, he rested his forehead on her back for a moment. Then he pulled out from her, and she lowered herself silently onto the bed. Beside her, he felt his erection shrivel.

Now the heavier caseload is not only failing to dampen his obsessive fantasies, it may even be encouraging them. Too often Will comes home in the dark to dinner eaten in solitude, to sex without conversation—sex with a sleepy (sometimes almost sleeping) wife, followed by however many laps of CNN it takes to put him to bed. Addicted to its repetition of headlines and looping tape feed, the astigmatic crawl of reprocessed information at the bottom of the screen, he finds it almost reassuring that news desks recycle crimes and atrocities. Apparently there aren't yet enough to fill twenty-four hours of broadcast.

For as far back as he can remember in his professional life, Will's days had proceeded, one after another, like the pages of a book, a text he found readable, sometimes engrossing, above all comprehensible. It was a book he understood. Then, abruptly, this orderly narrative—*his* orderly narrative, the book of Will—gave way to a wild scribbling of urges.

No, that's not true. It may seem he's come apart all at once, but it's an alignment—a compounding—of fractures, none of them new: estrangement from brother; death of son; reinvention of father. All versions of himself, if he can get away with such a Will-centered universe. Well, yes, of course he can. Inside his own head, he can. And why stop there? Why, when father, twin, and son cover all the tenses—past, present, and future? No wonder he was so . . . so whatever he was at the reunion. He's ceased to exist as an extension of himself.

Fuck! Yes, he's obsessed with sex. How else could he escape the inside of his head, where every thought refuses to be fleeting and instead waits its turn to be hyperarticulated, edited, revised, and then annotated like some nightmare hybrid of Talmudic commentary and Freudian case study? How else to jump out of his own skin except by fantasies of getting into someone else's?

In the course of one session with the depressed forty-something accountant, the one with the shapeless khaki skirts, Will was transformed from attentive analyst into what his mother must have meant by *sex maniac*, a term he hasn't heard her use for many years and one he used to find ridiculous, associating it with tabloid papers and true-crime magazines and foolish women who read about rape and secretly dream of it as overly zealous lovemaking. The accountant was sitting across from Will in the black leather chair that matched his couch when suddenly he was standing above her and she was on her knees begging to suck his cock. Not really, of course, and neither did they move on to frenzied, acrobatic-bordering-on-tantric sex.

Except that they did in his head. In his head they did.

He's used to the more or less constant nano-porn that buzzes through his male brain without overcoming or even disrupting the sequence of his thoughts. This is a fact of his mental life. But the new preoccupation is something different, leaving him at the mercy of ultralustful thoughts featuring whoever sits in the chair opposite his, or, worse, lies on his couch so she can't see that he is staring at her breasts. Objectively speaking, not one of the women he treats is as beautiful as his wife, not nearly. But whose fantasies are objective?

On his once rigorously exacting fuckability scale, on which even the iconic Pamela Anderson or J. Lo rated 9, every woman is now awarded 10 out of 10. Fat, thin, old, young, short, tall, dark, fair, flat, stacked: a perfect score depends on nothing more than being female.

The accountant, the grad student, even his training analysand. The menopausal one with too much money. The ASPCA officer, a typically misanthropic animal lover with white dog hair on her black sweaters. The archetypally unfulfilled tax lawyer who arrives for each session with a new missionary plan, off to Africa to adopt AIDS babies one week, bringing birth control to India the next. The lesbian who, having at last moved in with her partner, has decided she probably isn't gay after all. The bride-to-be who has not told her betrothed that she is infertile because her fallopian tubes were badly scarred by pelvic inflammatory disease contracted while she worked her way through college as a stripper who sometimes traded sex for money. The buxom one, who in the old days would have rated a good 7.5, maybe 8, and who makes everything that much worse by letting her snug skirt ride up her thighs and asking outright, "I am attractive, aren't I? I mean I do look good enough, don't I? Be honest with me, please. I know you're my therapist, Dr. Moreland, but as a man do you find me to be an attractive woman?" And all the rest of them.

They talk; he nods. He says "Oh," says "Hmm," says "Yes, I see what you mean," says "Please, go on. I think we should pursue this," and no matter who she is, no matter how inhibited or crazy or admittedly frigid, she's instantly made over into a sexpot whose only purpose is to gratify his every lustful wish.

At work these fantasies remain upbeat, but when he revisits a scenario later, as he inevitably does in his chronic insomnia, they sour with an almost film-noir relish for bad endings, a narrative free fall he's helpless to stop. It all comes apart in awful, bruising sex, intercourse that amounts to battery, struggles that arise out of the one irreversible law of Will's fantasies: there can be no blind consummations. No closed eyes, no doing it in the dark, no front to back, no sixty-nine, no anything that would prevent eye contact: this is the rule, the one point on which he won't—can't—compromise and the one point she can't—won't—accept.

As the forbidden interaction with his patient devolves from consensual to coerced, what he sees in his head acquires an increasingly sordid cast, transformed from the cheery Kodachrome of *Playboy* centerfolds to the grainy, indistinct black and white of crimes unfolding on the monitor of a closed-circuit camera, acts recorded by a secret, peering eye. Hiked-up skirts and yanked-down panty hose, spread thighs, wet whites of eyes, undergarments strewn on the floor: sufficiently arousing that even after having had sex with his wife Will can flog himself on to a second and sometimes (well, once) a third ejaculation. No top-flight orgasm, that third; it left him feeling dizzy and ruined. But he's forty-seven. Even hard-won prowess infuses him with something enough like optimism that he leaves his bed for a nearby armchair where he can move freely without disturbing his wife's sleep.

Typically, by the time Will arrives at orgasm his imagined partner has suffered the opposite of synergy; she's less than the sum of her parts, or fewer parts than would add up to a person: only lips, breasts, the downy cleft of her ass, the handful of flesh, so soft, inside the top of each thigh. It's only afterward, when he's spent and slumped in the chair, that both body and narrative reassemble. The same woman who began by begging for it reports Will's misconduct to the authorities, not some panel of toothless Ph.D.'s whose idea of discipline is re-analysis with the agenda of shrinking his libido back to manageable proportions, but real authorities, whose power is violence. Nameless, faceless storm troopers deliver him to a barricaded compound far from home and family, a place from which he cannot be rescued. There he is blindfolded, beaten, and stripped of his license, his reputation, his savings—all that twenty years of hard work have afforded him. Bound and gagged, with no expectation of release, he's left to bleed silently.

"Maybe," Will says to Daniel, "maybe I'm having a midlife crisis. What do you think?"

Daniel raises his white eyebrows. "Facile. That's what I think. Besides, didn't you already have a midlife crisis?"

"Did I? I don't think so."

"I was remembering the thing with Carole's sister."

"That wasn't a *thing*. And it wasn't *with*. It was an infatuation. Not consummated. Hardly a crisis. As I remember, I was so unnerved by my being attracted to Rachel that I ignored her to the point that she told Carole she thought I didn't like her. I had to work pretty hard to undo the damage I'd done."

Daniel picks up a heavy Mont Blanc pen from his desk, balancing it upright on the blotter between his thumb and index finger and sliding them all the way down the barrel until the pen falls, its end still caught between thumb and finger. He repeats the motion, over and over, and Will watches the way each time the pen falls, it hits the blotter with a little bounce.

"Will," Daniel says, "where did you go?"

"I don't know. Nowhere."

"Nowhere?"

"I guess I was trying to characterize for myself the emotions that go with the fantasies. What I feel. Or what I feel apart from lust."

"And?"

"Well, fear at the idea of being found out, caught in the act. And anger. Angry at myself for being so foolish. For risking so much to satisfy lust. But that anger is rational, after the fact. There's a more basic rage I can't get a handle on. Where does it come from? The lust itself is an angry lust, you know? Passion without tenderness. These are the nighttime scenarios I'm talking about. The fantasies during the day—the ones that distract me during a session with a patient—they're pretty uninteresting. Like *Penthouse* 'Forum' letters. Wishful, silly. But the nighttime stuff, it taps into this anguished rage I can't unpack.

"I mean, it's easy enough to admit that I'm angry with Carole about her having restricted our sex life. All those rules that kicked in after . . . after Luke." Will clears his throat, trying to prevent emotion from making his voice crack. "I think of it as her not allowing me to have sex with Luke's mother. Which I understand. I mean I'm not unaware of how profoundly everything is affected by a loss this . . . this big."

"Is that her explanation or yours?" Daniel asks, having waited for Will to compose himself.

"Mine. My explanation. Carole won't talk about it. If I bring any of this up, she accuses me of trying to turn her into one of my patients."

"Is she talking to anyone?"

"A therapist, you mean? No, no. She doesn't believe in it, not for herself. She believes in yoga. Yoga classes. Yoga books." Will sits forward in his chair. "Actually, we joke about it, but what Carole reads about isn't yoga. She'd say I was imposing meaning on what has no real significance, but she's addicted to this true-crime stuff—sinister, violent. Lust murders. Women savaged by misogynistic psychopaths. The kind of guys—you know the profile—whose mothers were prostitutes, or their sadistic fathers beat them, or there's a frontal-lobe injury or an organic brain disorder, or maybe it's idiopathic and they're just evil. Richard Speck. Ted Bundy. Sex and violence inextricably bound up. And the stories have to be true. He can't be a fictional monster. She couldn't care less about Hannibal Lecter.

"I get there's a fascination in being witness to a crime. I mean, probably the interest in most movies, novels, biographies—any narrative—depends on voyeurism, but this seems, well, maybe self-loathing is too strong a word. But suspect anyway. Driven by unconscious need. Otherwise why read one after another book about women getting raped and stabbed? Dismembered." Will shakes his head. "I think she herself worries they represent a perverse impulse, because she hides them. Even has one of those weird little fabric book-cover things so she can read them unnoticed in a waiting room or in front of Samantha. But she won't admit any contradiction in being a . . . a feminist and a yoga devotee and a purchaser of only organic produce, member of the food co-op, NYPIRG, Amnesty International, et cetera, as well as an insatiable consumer of true crime. With photo inserts of chopped-up women. And yes, I do realize that I've switched the focus from me to someone else."

"How is it," Daniel asks, "that Carole has figured out a way to refuse you sex with Luke's mother, as you say? In that Luke's mother is your wife."

"By arranging things so that I can get off with a female body, her body, but one she won't give a face. For three years now I've had to approach her from the back. She won't . . ."

"Won't what?" Daniel asks when Will doesn't finish the thought.

"She won't let me have missionary sex with her. Won't tolerate any position that might risk eye contact. Won't let me perform oral sex. Or touch her with my hand. She has orgasms, but I'm not allowed to give them to her. It's like I'm some guy who happens to be attached to the dildo she's using."

Daniel looks at Will closely. He's leaning forward over his desk, resting his chin on one hand. "You are angry," he says.

"Yes. Yes, I've said I am. But I keep feeling there's a piece missing from the explanations I've come up with. That it's too easy to assign blame to Luke's death. To call it a catalyst for every problem that develops between us."

"Still, you do find a connection between the violent fantasies about your patients and Carole's controlling your sex life? Limiting your access to her body?"

"Absolutely." Will frowns. "At least I think I do. Now, having mentioned her reading about serial killers immediately after talking about my violent sexual fantasies, I'm wondering if it's . . . if that's entirely coincidental. I guess it is—what connection could there be?—but then I worry that my tendency to insist upon connections leads me to find significance where there isn't any. Create meanings that don't exist outside of my consciousness. You know, the whole God thing."

"The God thing?"

"Yes, yes. The trap I fall into. Looking everywhere for significance. It gets out of my ability to control or direct it, won't remain within the boundary of my work, within my patient relationships. Suddenly, significance becomes signs. And there I am, back to obsessing over the possibility of God. Whether God exists or is merely projection. Whether the significance I find or the signs I see represent nothing more than my wish for meaning, or have a validity beyond my desires and my consciousness."

"Will," Daniel says. "Here's a place where I'm afraid I have to be textbook. Call attention to what you already know."

"Wait, wait." Will holds up his hand, laughing. Almost laughing. Every time he does laugh in Daniel's company he's aware, as he didn't use to be, of how similar it feels to crying. The rhythm of it, the way it tightens in his chest, stretches his face. "I heard it, too. I know what you're going to say."

"Tell me."

"My use of the word *obsessing* to characterize my thinking about God." Daniel nods. "I know, I know." Will's voice assumes the bored tone of rote repetition, with a little twist, a lilt, of self-parody. "What is it I'm trying so hard not to perceive? What is it that my obsession defends me against?"

"Exactly." Daniel replaces his pen in the leather tray next to his pipe stand. Though it's been many years since he's smoked, he keeps his pipes on his desk. Sometimes, while Will talks, he takes one and fiddles with it, using a handkerchief to polish its bowl, or holding it, empty, between his teeth, and Will knows these aren't the idle acts they seem but a conscious attempt to disarm him, to suggest the older man isn't listening as closely as he is.

"Remember when I asked if you considered psychoanalysis a type of conversion experience?" Will says.

"Remind me."

"It was a long time ago, years ago. I'd reached a moment of exultation, very excited about what we were doing because suddenly everything was illuminated. Flooded with light. I couldn't separate my . . . well, it was a form of ecstasy, and I didn't separate it from what would be described as a religious experience, scales dropping from before my eyes, however you want to describe it. And I asked didn't you think psychoanalysis was a religion as much as a science? It was a faith, Freud was a prophet, training analysis the conversion experience—a dramatic, road-to-Damascus-caliber revelation."

"What was my answer?" Daniel says.

"I don't know. I was so delighted with the question—really an observation couched as a question—that if you disagreed with me, I doubt I'd have heard you."

Will and Daniel stand, Will noting, not for the first time, that he and Daniel wear almost identical glasses, rimless bifocals with pewter-colored stems. Daniel fastens the middle button of his suit jacket. He holds his hand out to take Will's. "Next week?"

"Next week," Will agrees, comforted by the promise of speaking with Daniel again soon, even though these sessions don't seem to be helping. At least not with respect to the forbidden fantasies—the fantasies Will wants to forbid. They haven't lessened the frequency or the virulence of his lust attacks at all.

Increasingly, Will worries he'll succumb to what he'd reassure a patient was an innocuous normal outlet, and not the symptom of some monstrous psychopathology. He'd remind the hypothetical patient that even the most civilized gentlemen have their brutal fantasies. Especially the most civilized.

But Will isn't his own patient. He isn't hypothetical. What he is, is afraid. He doesn't feel he knows himself anymore, and it seems only a matter of time before he's no longer daydreaming but acting. Before he becomes the very thing he fears: a portion of unhappiness and ill fortune for the people he loves, the family he wants, brick by brick, to protect.

I t was two months or more after the reunion that Will e-mailed Elizabeth to apologize. He hadn't intended to put it off so long, but the wording kept tripping him up; he wrote draft after draft that he never sent. *Please forgive me,* he'd begin, typically, *or at least understand my ill-advised request.* Then he'd pause, delete *ill-advised,* or *foolish,* or *ridiculous,* whichever he'd chosen, put it back in, take it out, try to come up with a better word, fail, continue, *as proceeding from the context. I find such events disorienting, and it seems that a couple of glasses of wine were sufficient to enflame my imagination. You have my word that I will not pursue the matter we discussed. Best, Will.* He'd read it over, change a few words, change the last sentence. *You have my word that, though I remain interested in the question of your daughter's paternity, I will not attempt to contact her.* He'd change it back, delete the letter in its entirety, write another that was, but for a few articles and commas, identical to the first.

Finally, one day, it was already September, after a lengthening pause during which he wasn't so much thinking as staring, he hit the send button.

She hasn't replied. Not after a week, not after a month. Of course, he should never have voiced what was, he understood too late, a fantasy. A mistake to have mentioned anything about hair to Elizabeth. He blew it, and undoubtedly this was for the best. So why does he continue to check the mail so assiduously? Why, after more than a month of silence, is he still waiting to hear from Elizabeth? Thinking about making love to her? Well, not love. *Plank* would be the word. It's with pleasure that he imagines himself planking Elizabeth, changing the expression on her face from one of self-satisfaction to . . . to what? Astonishment. The one indelibly delightful memory of the reunion was the look on her face when he suggested she mail him one of her daughter's hairs.

For most of his professional life, Will has preferred working with women patients, who generally articulate their feelings more intelligently than men and whose emotional lives are more available to examination. But now it's the male patients upon whom he depends for relief. No matter that their progress is slow, their insights infrequent. At least he doesn't want to jump their bones. Three of his five new patients are men who have added their voices to what often strikes Will as the attenuated morality play of his work, a sprawling, incontinent production that could be titled "The Seven Deadly Sins." Replete with crises and lacking a resolution, this drama energetically addresses anger, sloth, avarice, and gluttony, ignores vanity and pride (if he had to choose whether this reflects his particular moment in history or the nature of psychoanalysis, he'd go with the former), and showcases lust.

"I love her," the guilt-riddled womanizer tells him. "I do love her. She thinks I can't love her and screw other women, but she's wrong. And it's not like we don't have great sex. Twenty years, and we're still hot for each other."

"So it isn't a matter of turning to other women for what your wife won't give you?"

"No, it's a matter of . . . I don't know what it's a matter of. But in the moment, when I'm with a woman, any woman, it's as if—this is preposterous, but at that moment I'm convinced that if I don't have sex with whoever it is, I'll never be able to get it up again. So, even though I'm aware that I'm sabotaging my marriage and maybe even my whole family, I can't not do it. It's compulsory, and not just from the point at which I'm in bed with whoever she is, but from the moment the idea of sex with that woman comes into my head. It's like the old expression 'Use it or lose it' has turned into some kind of spell, or curse. I end up screwing all kinds of women I don't even want to, when I don't want to."

He keeps talking even though he's seen Will look at his watch. "I've tried other things—everything," he says. "Acupuncture. Hypnosis. We've gone to couples therapy. Nothing works."

"Use it or lose it?" Will asks. The hour's up, but finally it seems as if they're on to something.

The man nods. "I even hear it in my head," he says. "Well, I hear a lot of things like that, phrases that get stuck in my head."

"Tell me about them."

The man shrugs self-consciously. "Some just bug me," he says, "like that old 'Step on a crack, break your mother's back.' And the other one that always pops up when I walk outside. As soon as I see dog crap, I hear 'Eat shit and die.' Well, obviously I don't act on that, but the words stay in my head. They play over and over until something, I don't know what, distracts me or turns them off somehow. I can't tell you how they stop because as long as I'm trying to turn them off, I can't, you know? They have to stop when I've given up, when I'm not paying attention anymore."

"Are there others of these directives?" Will asks. "Others you can remember?"

"Oh, yes, many of them. There's 'Haste makes waste' and 'A stitch in time'—things like that. 'No pain, no gain.'"

"Sayings, you mean? Aphorisms?"

"Yes. But while most of them bother me by repeating over and over, the 'Use it or lose it' one forces me to act because the idea that it's true, that I will lose it, is so powerful."

"Do you avoid cracks in the sidewalk?"

"I guess I do, yes."

"Do some of these directives occur more frequently than others?"

"No. At least I don't think they do."

"And mostly they stop when you obey?"

"Yes. I hadn't spelled it out that way to myself, but you're right."

Will makes a note. He's allowed the new patient to use up not only the few remaining minutes of his hour—he's never been one for forcing a fifty-minute break-off—but a little of the next patient's as well, and she comes in glaring at him. It's six minutes past.

"Maria," he says, standing to greet her. "Please forgive me. The . . . the gentleman whose appointment was immediately before yours was describing a complicated set of circumstances. You know I don't like to cut people off."

She nods, looking slightly mollified. "It's okay, I guess."

"Please," he says. He gestures toward the couch. "I was hoping that today, as I have a cancellation following your session, we could run overtime. If your schedule allows, that is."

"Yeah, thanks, okay." She hangs her coat in the closet but keeps her purse with her, lies down holding it in front of her crotch. Several times, she has pointed this habit out to Will, as if afraid he hasn't picked up on this self-conscious Freudian allusion. He never takes the bait when she asks him what it might mean, just lobs the question back at her.

"I feel like you're always watching me," she says as soon as she's comfortably settled.